My Dad,

Everyone's

Soldier

Tiera Rozman

Beaver's Pond Press, Inc.
Edina, Minnesota

T5-DHH-702

MY DAD, EVERYONE'S SOLDIER © copyright 2003 by Tiera Rozman. All rights reserved. No part of this book may be reproduced in any form whatsoever, by photography or xerography or by any other means, by broadcast or transmission, by translation into any kind of language, nor by recording electronically or otherwise, without permission in writing from the author, except by a reviewer, who may quote brief passages in critical articles or reviews.

ISBN 1-59298-009-0

Book design and typesetting: Mori Studio

Printed in the United States of America

First Printing: April 2003

07 06 05 04 03   6 5 4 3 2 1

Beaver's Pond Press, Inc.

7104 Ohms Lane, Suite 216
Edina, MN 55439
(952) 829-8818
www.BeaversPondPress.com

To order, visit *www.BookHouseFulfillment.com* or call
1-800-901-3480. Reseller discounts available.

Acknowledgements

My heart goes out to all of the families whose loved ones have been called to duty. Your sacrifice and dedication to our country is appreciated more than words can tell.

I would like to thank Tiffany and Kaiden for the inspiration behind this story and most importantly to Matt, whose dedication to his family and our freedom will not be forgotten.

I would also like to thank my husband and two children for all their support and mostly their love.

My Dad was shipped out.
My mom cried.
So did I.

Now my dad is a soldier, yesterday he was a reserve. That means he used to be a soldier once a month, but they ran out of regular army people so they had to call my dad. Now he's not just my dad, he's everyone's soldier.

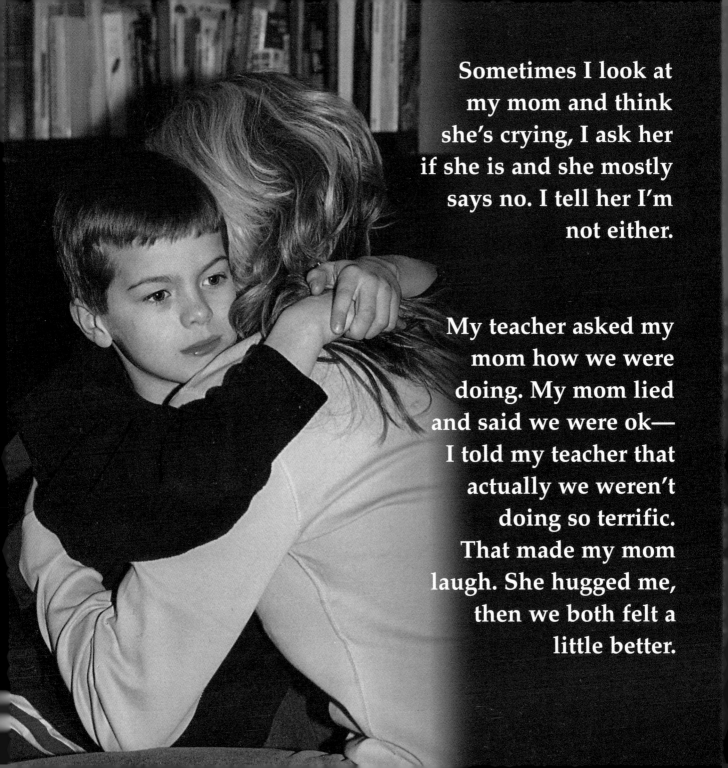

Sometimes I look at my mom and think she's crying, I ask her if she is and she mostly says no. I tell her I'm not either.

My teacher asked my mom how we were doing. My mom lied and said we were ok— I told my teacher that actually we weren't doing so terrific. That made my mom laugh. She hugged me, then we both felt a little better.

I gave my dad some candy—I snuck it into his bag before he left. I think he will probably remember me when he eats it and that will make him happy.

They gave my dad a shot in the butt, it hurt so he couldn't sit down. Even though he is a soldier that doesn't mean he likes needles.

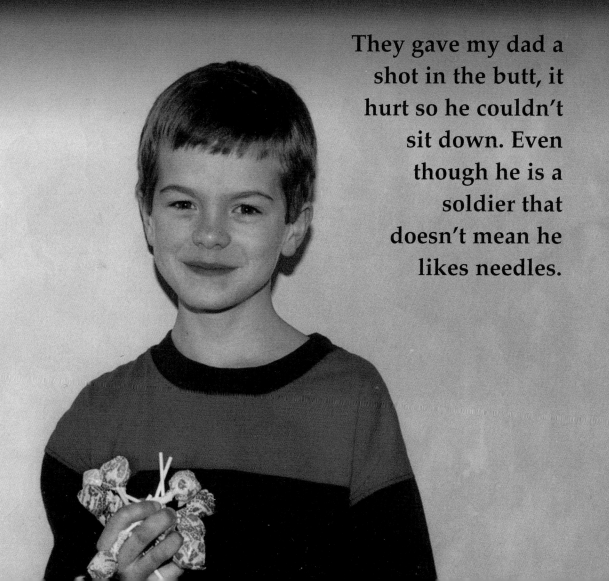

He is going to be gone past my birthday
and his birthday too.

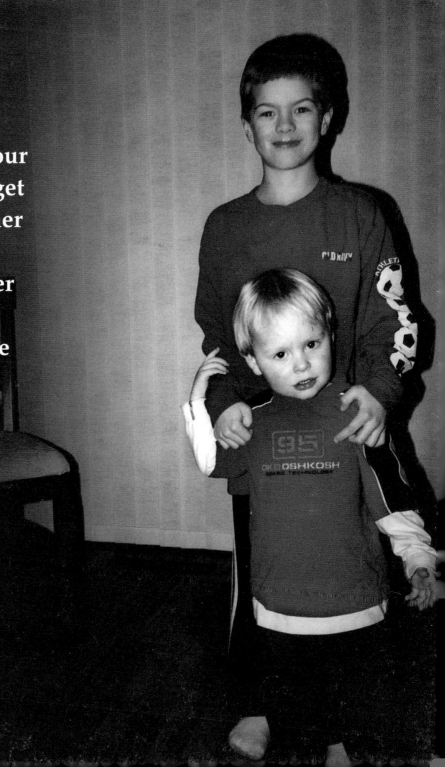

I show my baby brother pictures of our dad so he won't forget who he is. My brother kisses his picture everyday. My brother calls out to my dad when we walk in the door, but he doesn't answer.

My dad made us a video tape so he could be with us every night by reading us a story before we go to bed. My dad thinks we might forget him if he's gone too long. I think I'll miss him everyday.

My dad is brave and nice. He helps me when I'm hurt.
He can fix anything. I like playing with him.
I always win when we play pool.

My favorite thing
about my dad is
mostly everything.
He's nice.

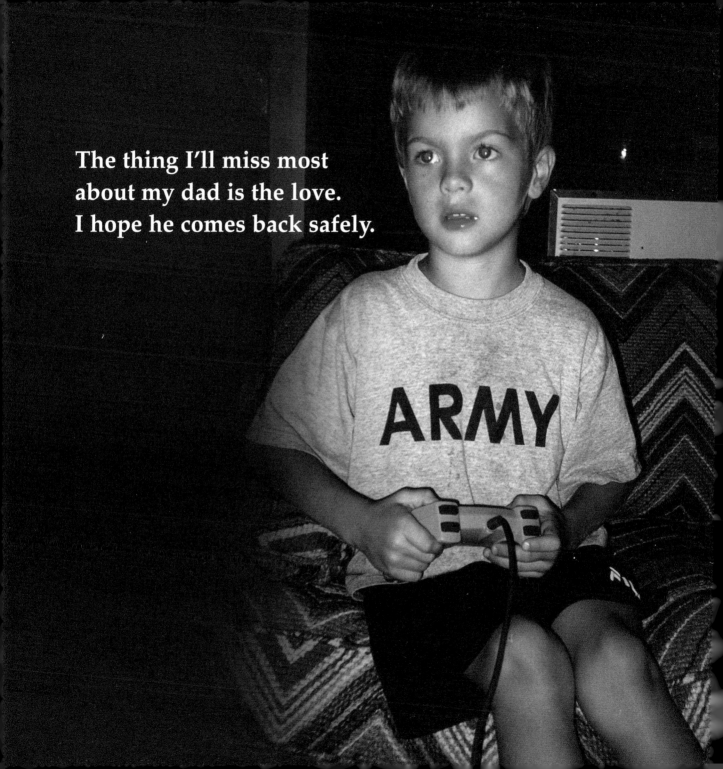

The thing I'll miss most about my dad is the love. I hope he comes back safely.

The first thing I'm going to do when I see him is hug and kiss him, and then I'm going to tell him I didn't forget him.

Dear Dad,

I miss you so much and I love you so much. I hope you are having a good time. I was crying for you today. Can you send a E-mail to me or a letter? Collin made a letter for you on this paper. I wish you were here then that would be a miracle. Lots of people supported you, choir the school and church the family too. Remember God and Jesus are watching over you. It is snowing where we are. I'll talk to you later bye.

by Kaiden
Collin and mom
I LOVE You.

This is my Family.

Happy.